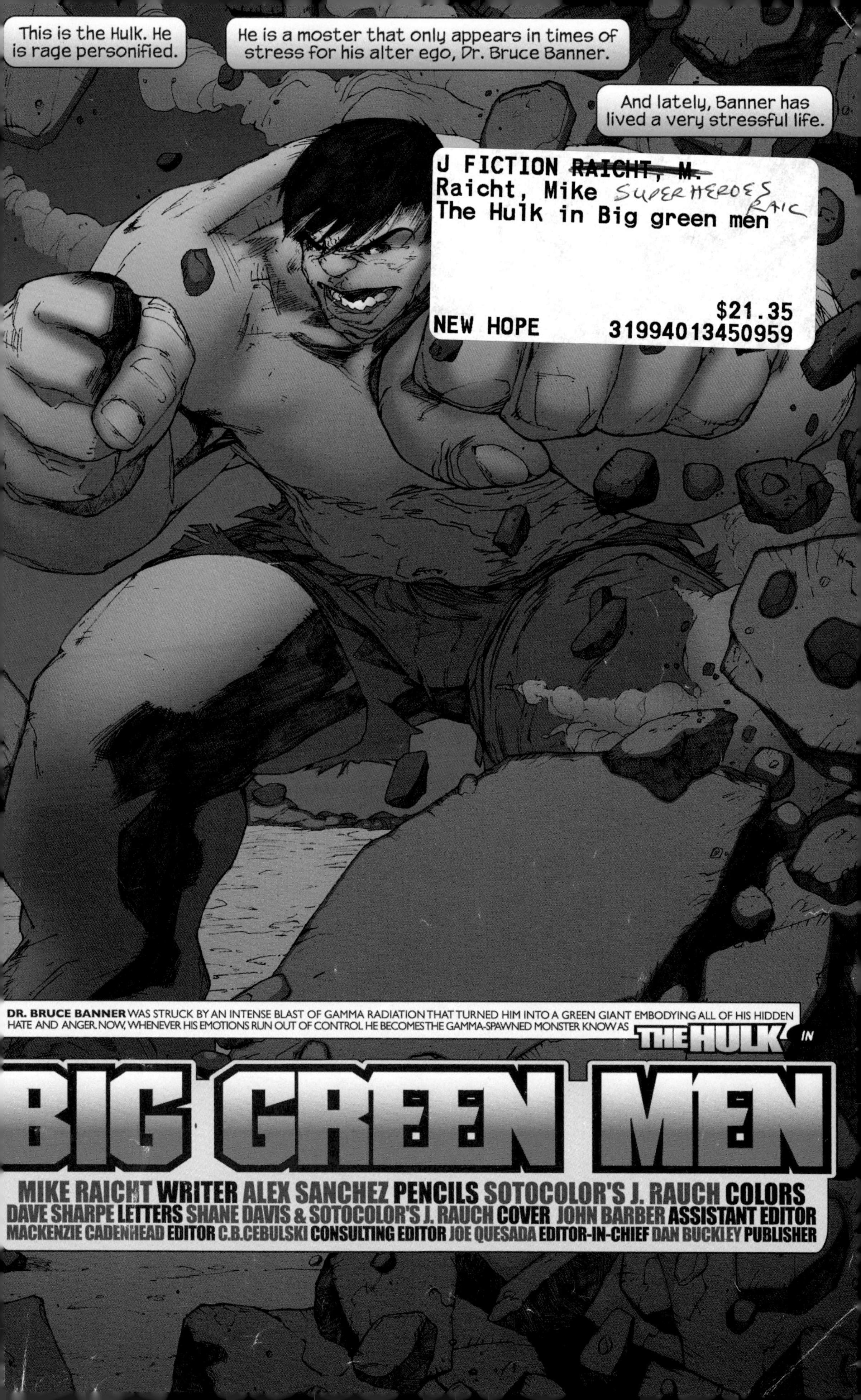
This is the Hulk. He is rage personified.
He is a moster that only appears in times of stress for his alter ego, Dr. Bruce Banner.
And lately, Banner has lived a very stressful life.
DR. BRUCE BANNER WAS STRUCK BY AN INTENSE BLAST OF GAMMA RADIATION THAT TURNED HIM INTO A GREEN GIANT EMBODYING ALL OF HIS HIDDEN HATE AND ANGER. NOW, WHENEVER HIS EMOTIONS RUN OUT OF CONTROL HE BECOMES THE GAMMA-SPAWNED MONSTER KNOW AS THE HULK IN
BIG GREEN MEN
MIKE RAICHT WRITER ALEX SANCHEZ PENCILS SOTOCOLOR'S J. RAUCH COLORS
DAVE SHARPE LETTERS SHANE DAVIS & SOTOCOLOR'S J. RAUCH COVER JOHN BARBER ASSISTANT EDITOR
MACKENZIE CADENHEAD EDITOR C.B.CEBULSKI CONSULTING EDITOR JOE QUESADA EDITOR-IN-CHIEF DAN BUCKLEY PUBLISHER

VISIT US AT
www.abdopub.com

Spotlight, a division of ABDO Publishing Company Inc., is the school and library distributor of the Marvel Entertainment books.

Library of Congress Cataloging-in-Publication Data

Raicht, Mike.
The Hulk in Big green men / Mike Raicht, writer ; Alex Sanchez, pencils ; J. Rauch, colors ; Dave Sharpe, letters ; Shane Davis & J. Rauch, cover.
p. cm.
"Marvel age"—Cover.
Revision of a Jan. 2005 issue of Incredible Hulk.
ISBN 1-59961-042-6
1. Graphic novels. I. Sanchez, Alex. II. Incredible Hulk (New York, N.Y. : 1999) III. Title.

PN 6728.H8R34 2006
741.5'973—dc22

2005057558

All Spotlight books are reinforced library binding
and manufactured in the United States of America

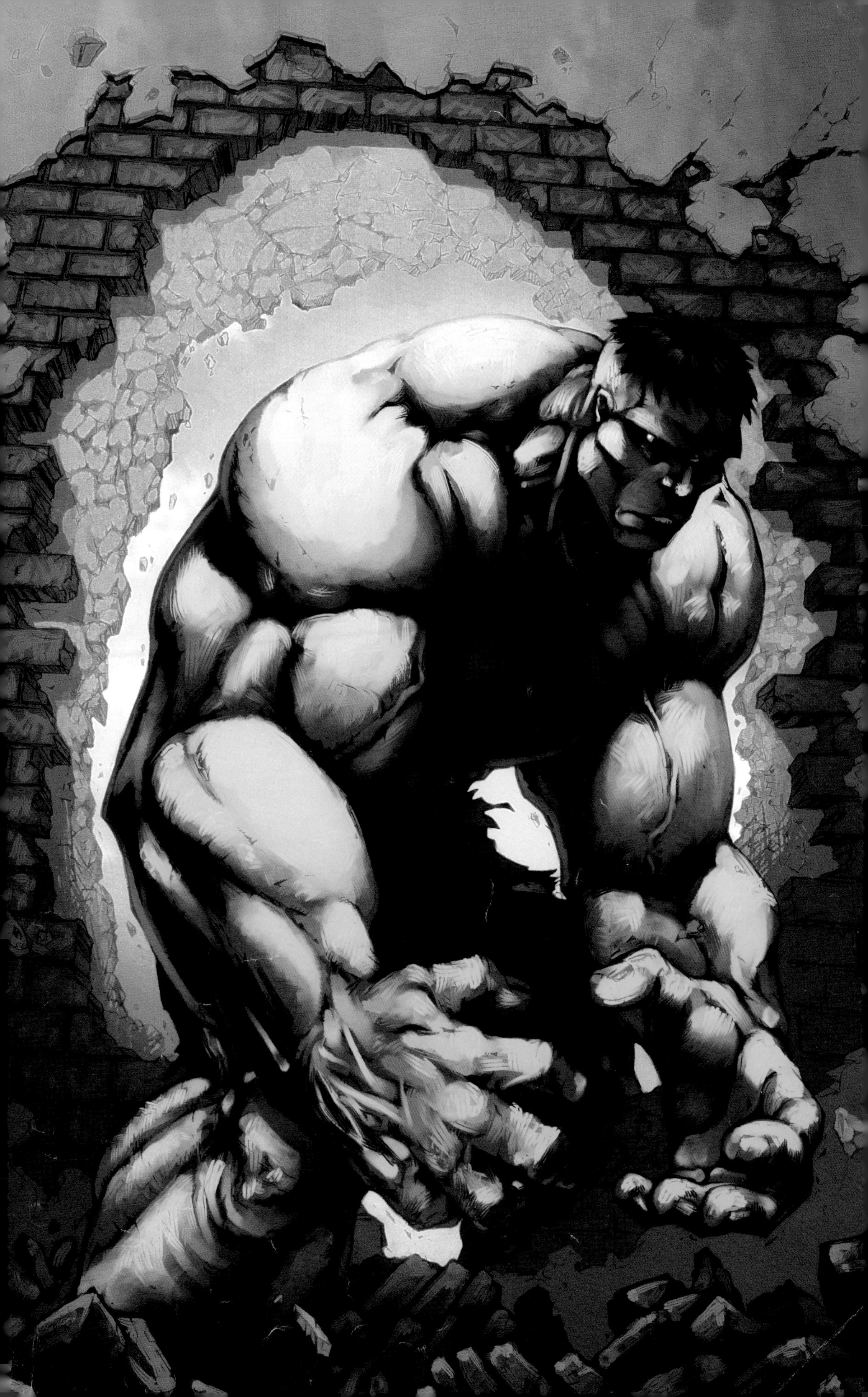

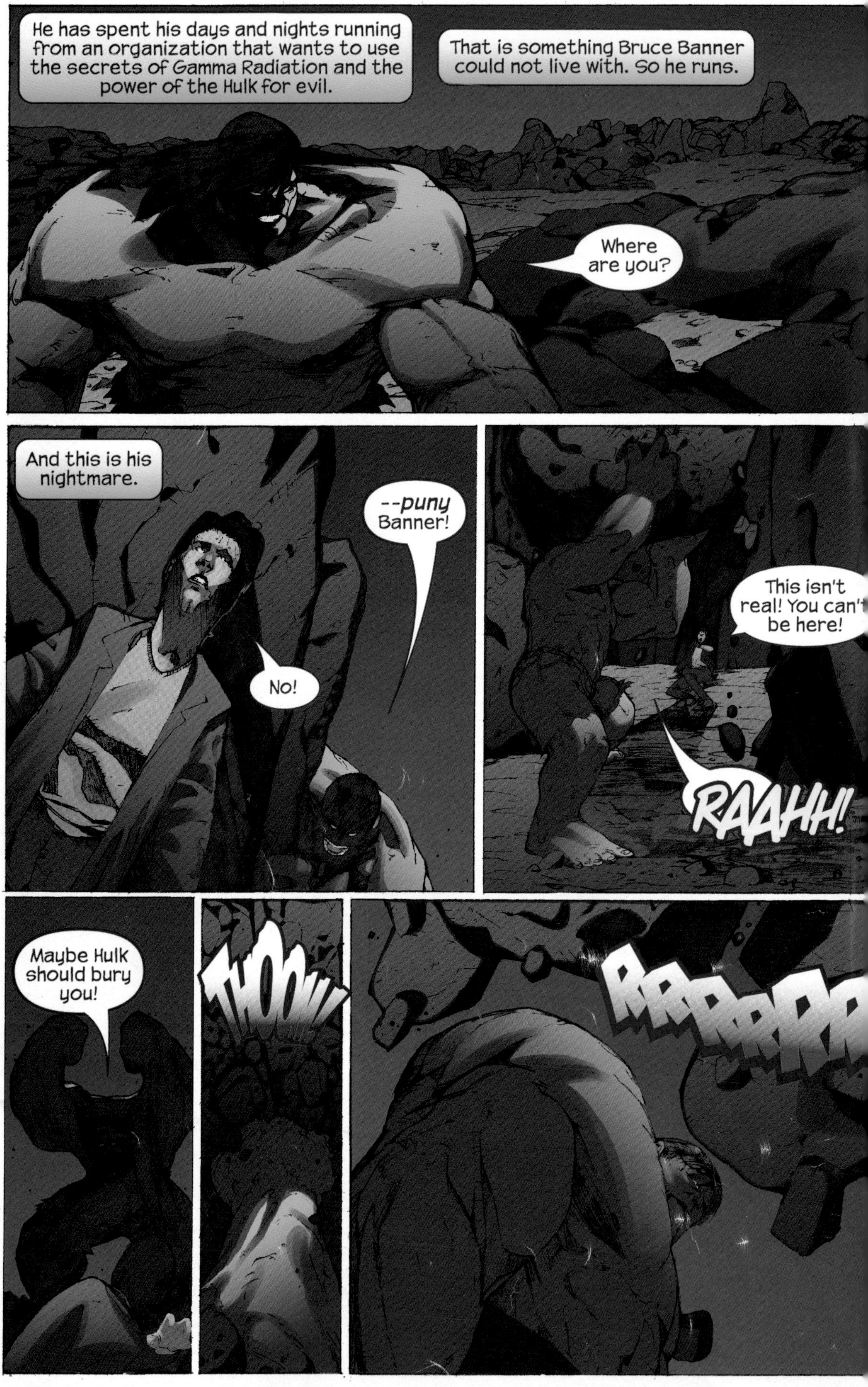
He has spent his days and nights running from an organization that wants to use the secrets of Gamma Radiation and the power of the Hulk for evil.
That is something Bruce Banner could not live with. So he runs.
Where are you?
And this is his nightmare.
--puny Banner!
No!
This isn't real! You can't be here!
RAAHH!
Maybe Hulk should bury you!
THOOM!
RRRRRRR

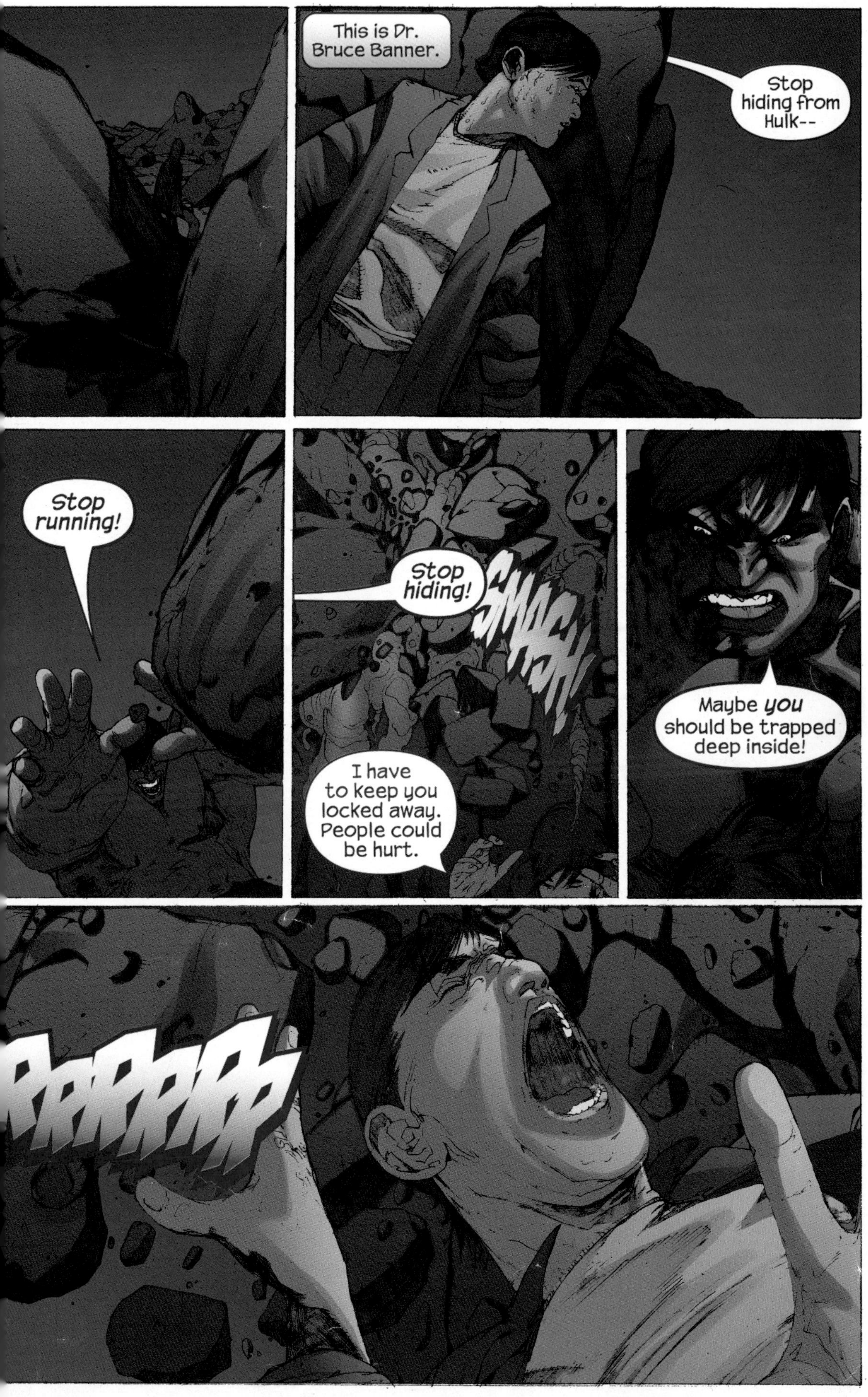
This is Dr. Bruce Banner.
Stop hiding from Hulk--
Stop running!
Stop hiding!
SMASH
I have to keep you locked away. People could be hurt.
Maybe you should be trapped deep inside!
RRRRRR

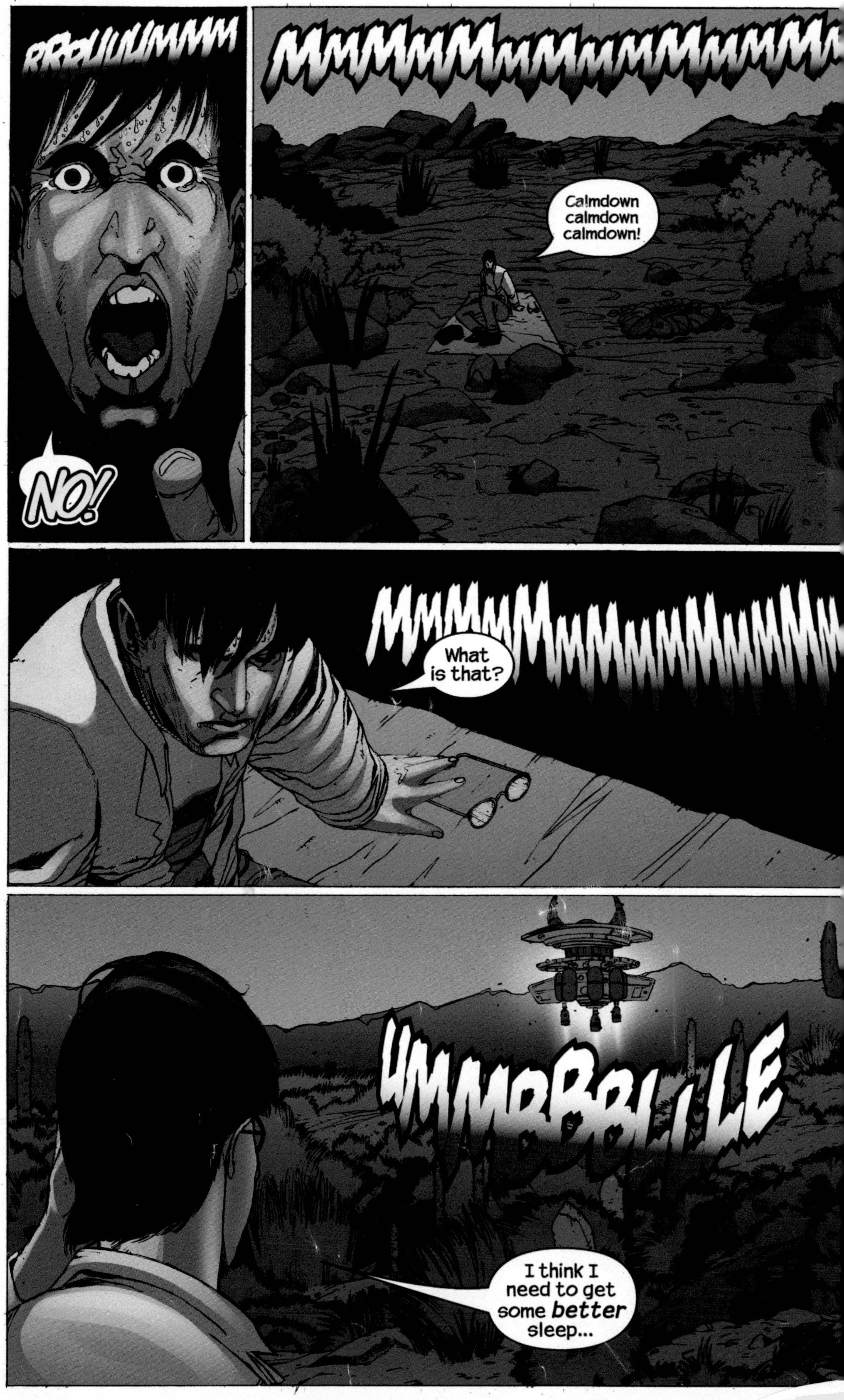
NO!
Calmdown calmdown calmdown!
What is that?
I think I need to get some *better* sleep...

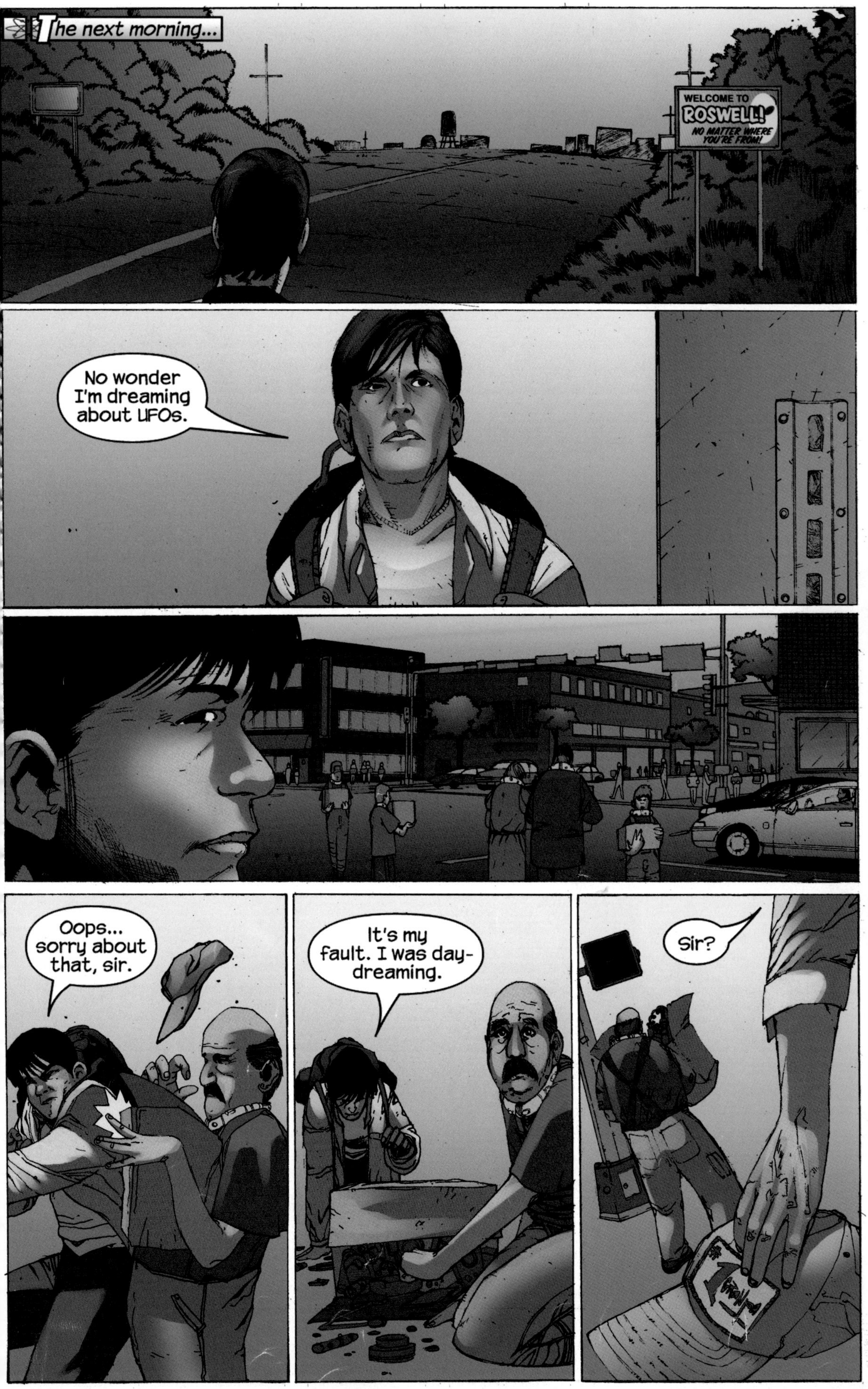
The next morning...
WELCOME TO
ROSWELL!
NO MATTER WHERE YOU'RE FROM!
No wonder I'm dreaming about UFOs.
Oops... sorry about that, sir.
It's my fault. I was day-dreaming.
Sir?

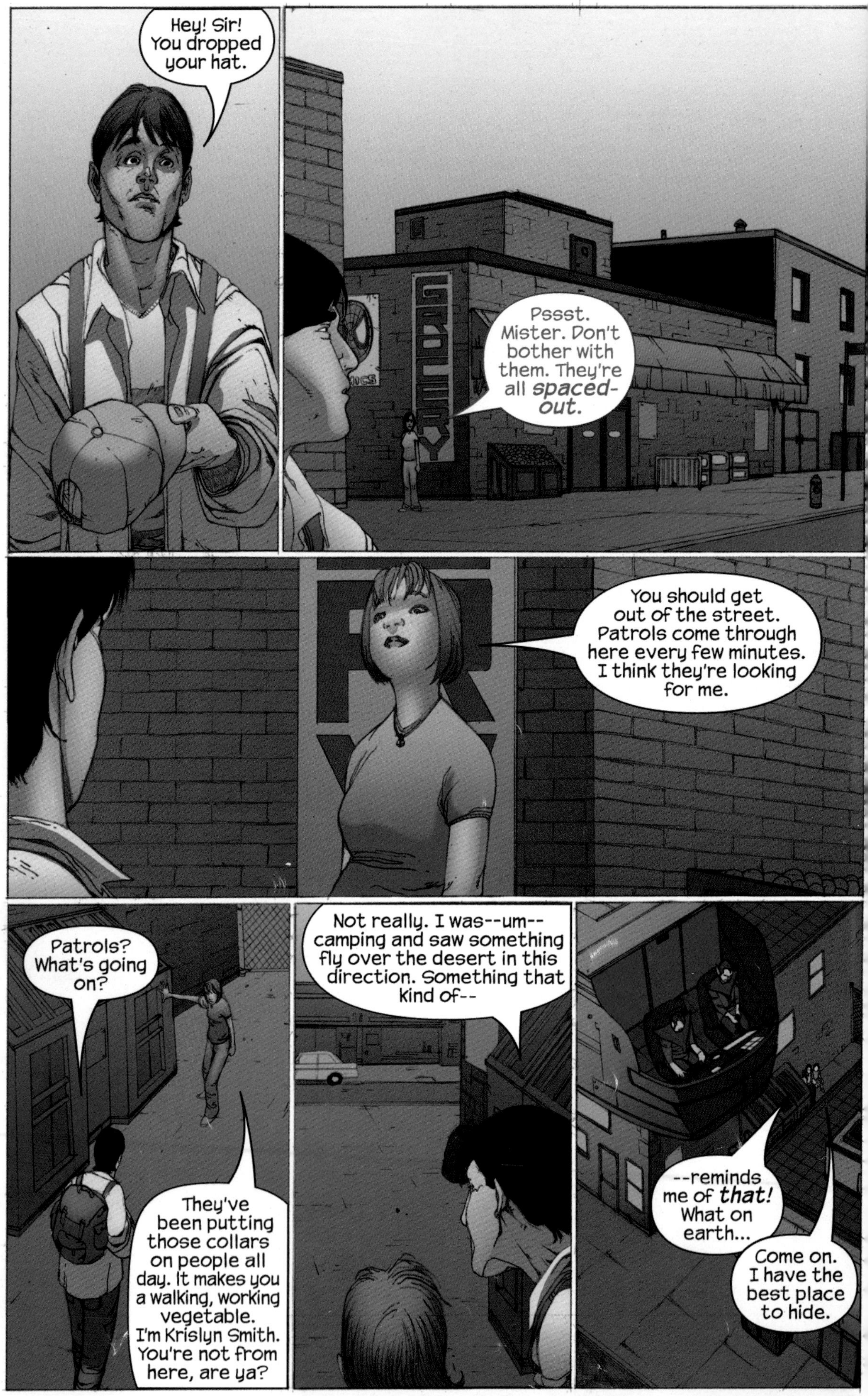

Hey! Sir! You dropped your hat.
Pssst. Mister. Don't bother with them. They're all *spaced-out*.
You should get out of the street. Patrols come through here every few minutes. I think they're looking for me.
Patrols? What's going on?
They've been putting those collars on people all day. It makes you a walking, working vegetable. I'm Krislyn Smith. You're not from here, are ya?
Not really. I was--um--camping and saw something fly over the desert in this direction. Something that kind of--
--reminds me of *that!* What on earth...
Come on. I have the best place to hide.

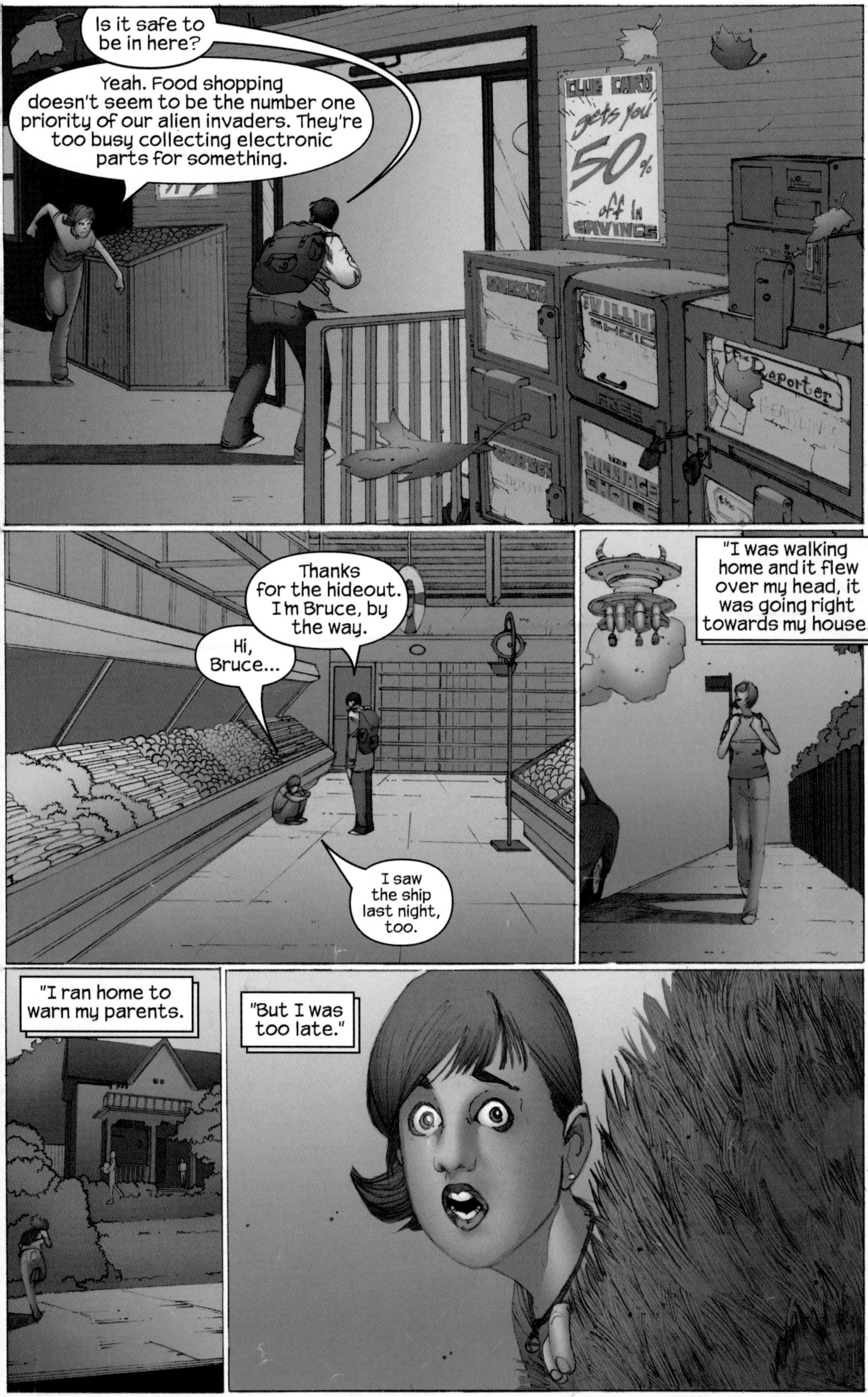
Is it safe to be in here?
Yeah. Food shopping doesn't seem to be the number one priority of our alien invaders. They're too busy collecting electronic parts for something.
CLUB CARD gets you 50% off in SAVINGS
The Reporter
Thanks for the hideout. I'm Bruce, by the way.
Hi, Bruce...
I saw the ship last night, too.
"I was walking home and it flew over my head, it was going right towards my house.
"I ran home to warn my parents.
"But I was too late."

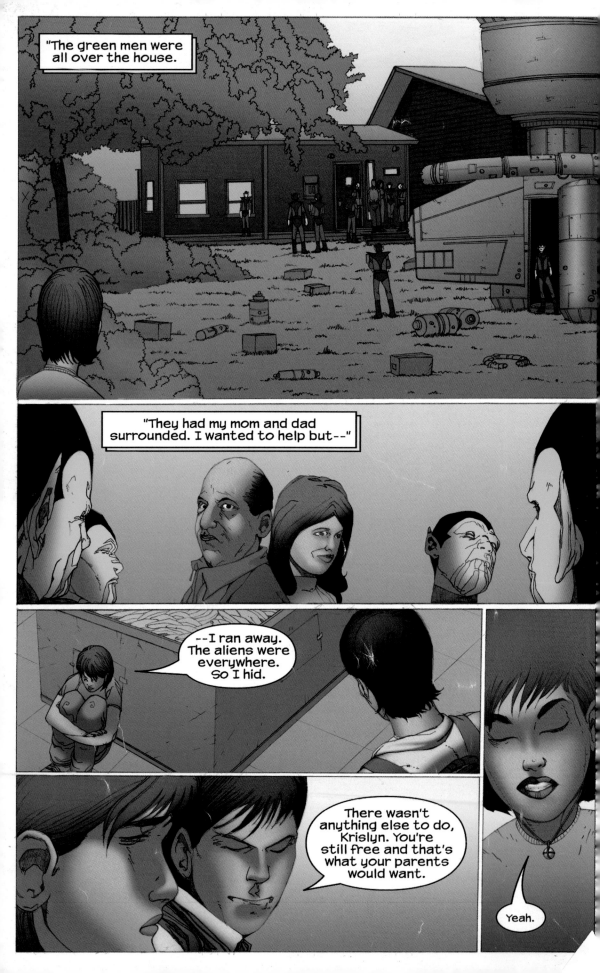

"The green men were all over the house.

"They had my mom and dad surrounded. I wanted to help but--"

--I ran away. The aliens were everywhere. So I hid.

There wasn't anything else to do, Krislyn. You're still free and that's what your parents would want.

Yeah.

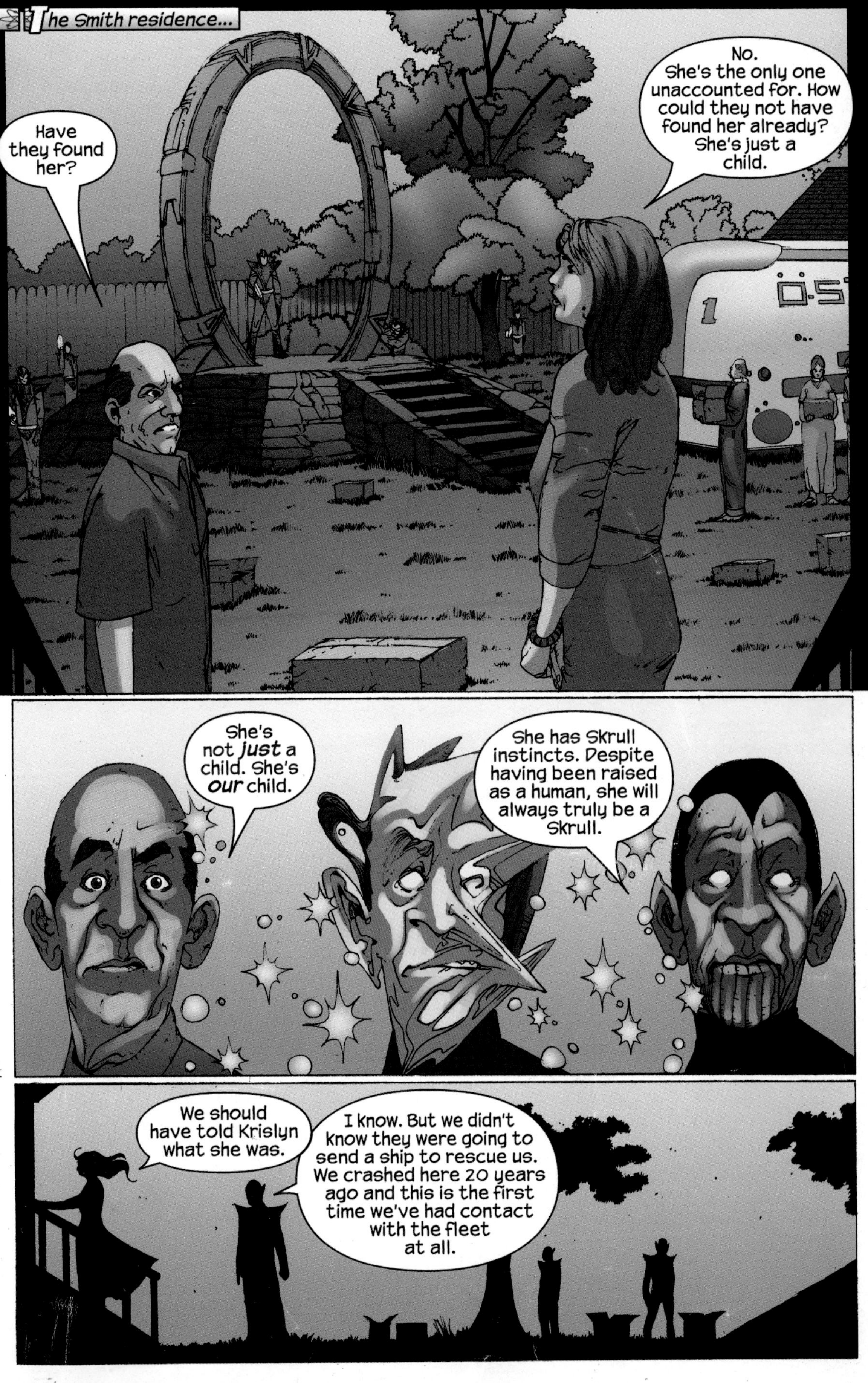
The Smith residence...
Have they found her?
No. She's the only one unaccounted for. How could they not have found her already? She's just a child.
She's not *just* a child. She's *our* child.
She has Skrull instincts. Despite having been raised as a human, she will always truly be a Skrull.
We should have told Krislyn what she was.
I know. But we didn't know they were going to send a ship to rescue us. We crashed here 20 years ago and this is the first time we've had contact with the fleet at all.

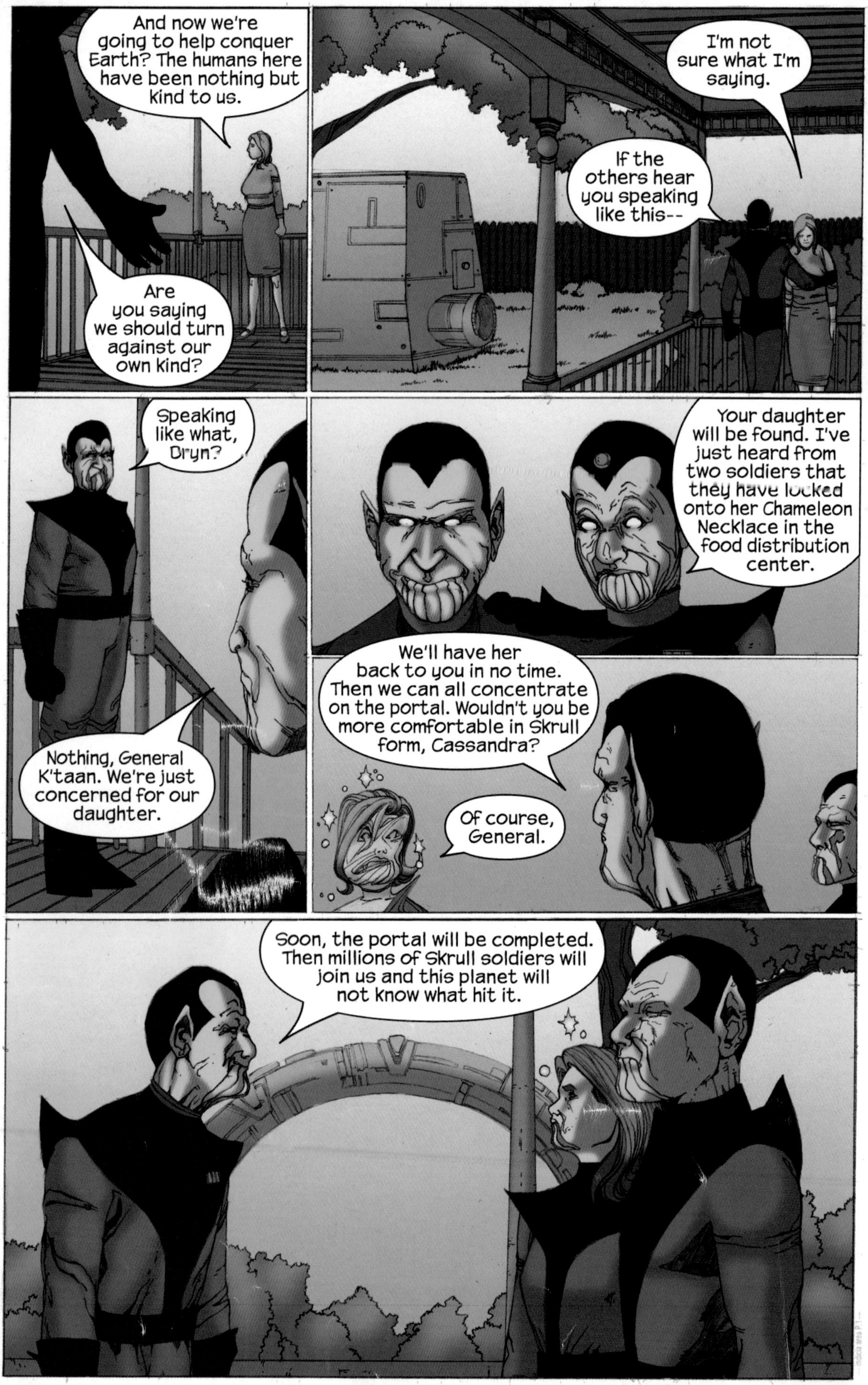
And now we're going to help conquer Earth? The humans here have been nothing but kind to us.
Are you saying we should turn against our own kind?
I'm not sure what I'm saying.
If the others hear you speaking like this--
Speaking like what, Dryn?
Nothing, General K'taan. We're just concerned for our daughter.
Your daughter will be found. I've just heard from two soldiers that they have locked onto her Chameleon Necklace in the food distribution center.
We'll have her back to you in no time. Then we can all concentrate on the portal. Wouldn't you be more comfortable in Skrull form, Cassandra?
Of course, General.
Soon, the portal will be completed. Then millions of Skrull soldiers will join us and this planet will not know what hit it.

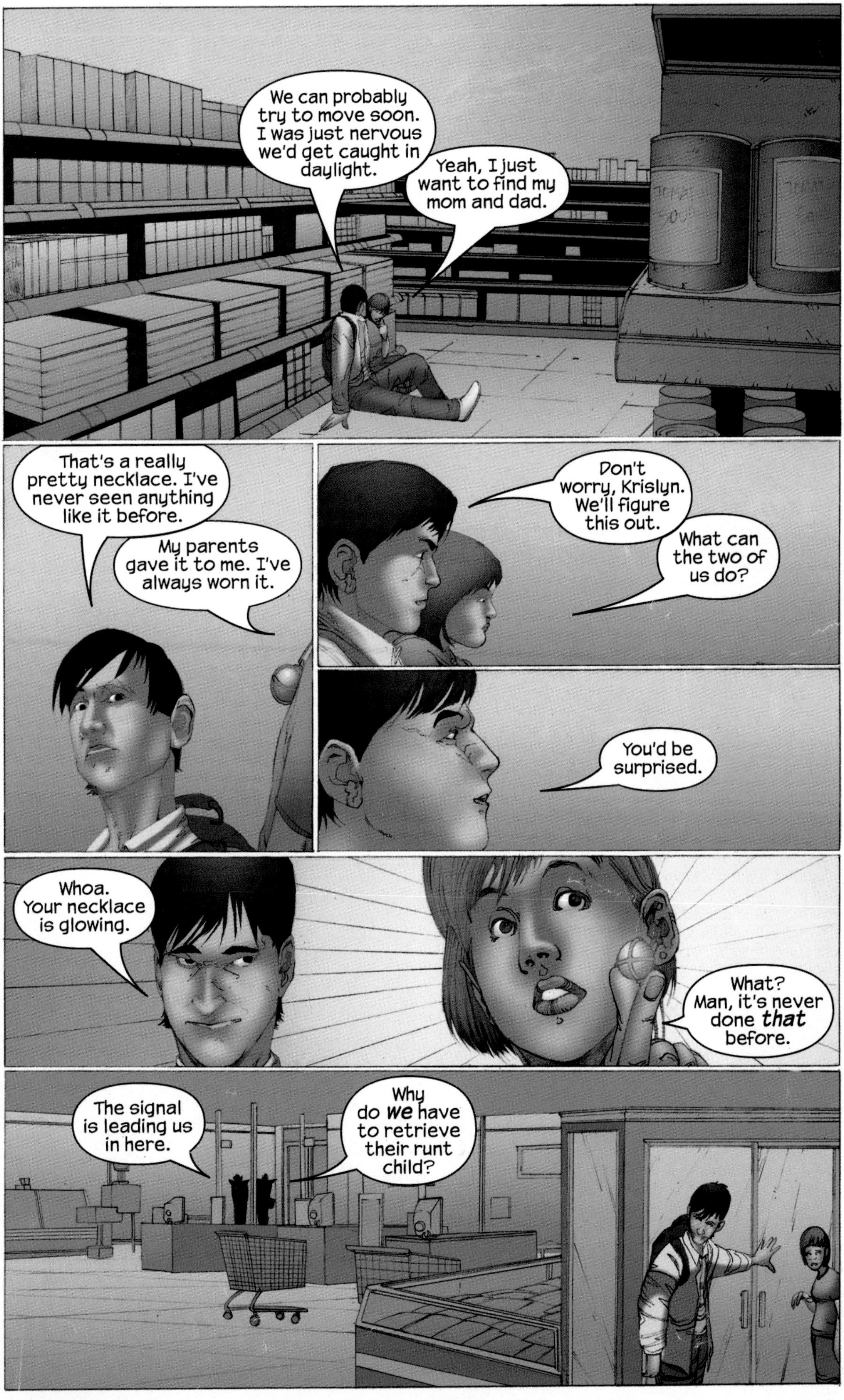
We can probably try to move soon. I was just nervous we'd get caught in daylight.
Yeah, I just want to find my mom and dad.
That's a really pretty necklace. I've never seen anything like it before.
My parents gave it to me. I've always worn it.
Don't worry, Krislyn. We'll figure this out.
What can the two of us do?
You'd be surprised.
Whoa. Your necklace is glowing.
What? Man, it's never done *that* before.
The signal is leading us in here.
Why do *we* have to retrieve their runt child?

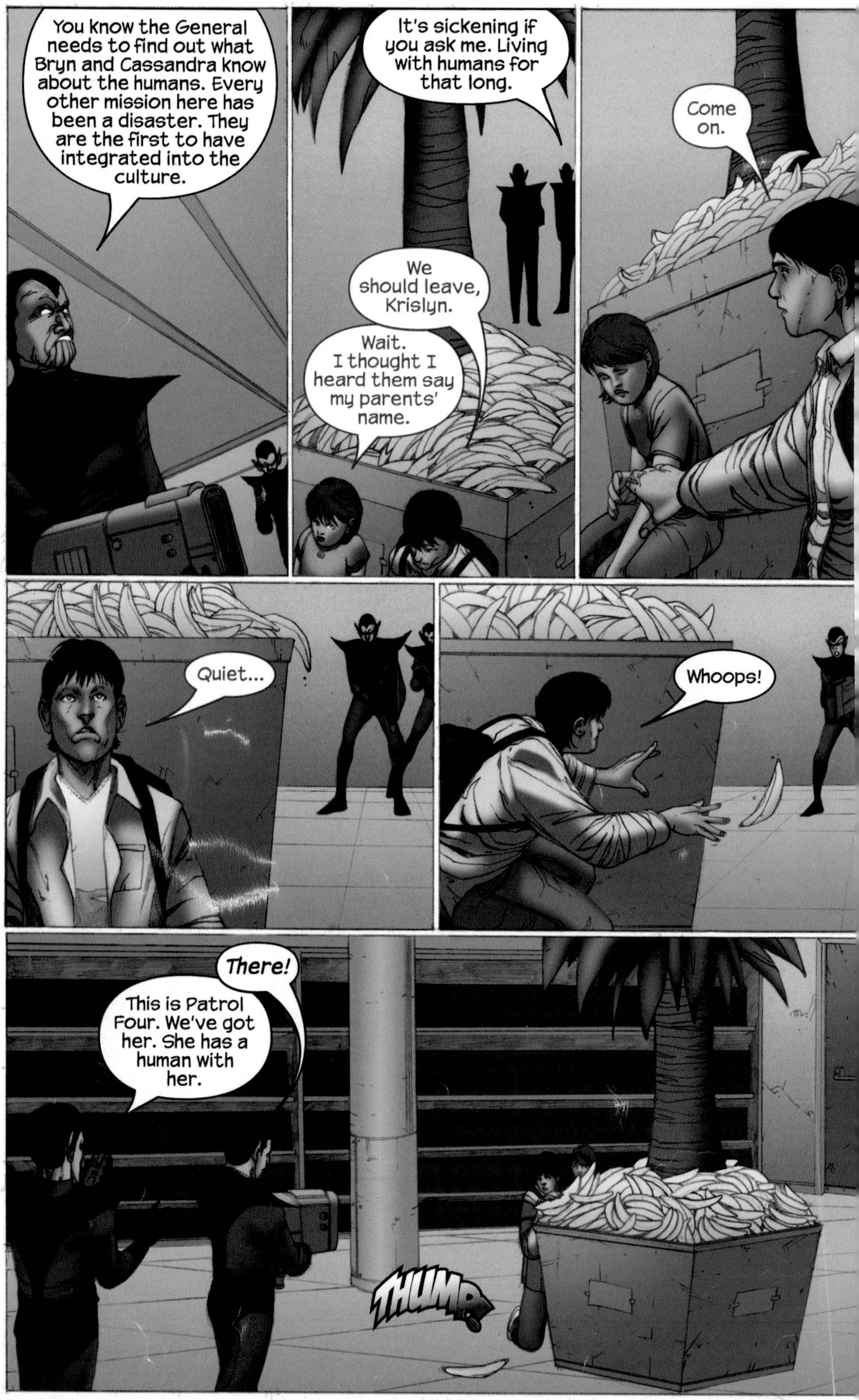
You know the General needs to find out what Bryn and Cassandra know about the humans. Every other mission here has been a disaster. They are the first to have integrated into the culture.
It's sickening if you ask me. Living with humans for that long.
We should leave, Krislyn.
Wait. I thought I heard them say my parents' name.
Come on.
Quiet...
Whoops!
There!
This is Patrol Four. We've got her. She has a human with her.
THUMP!

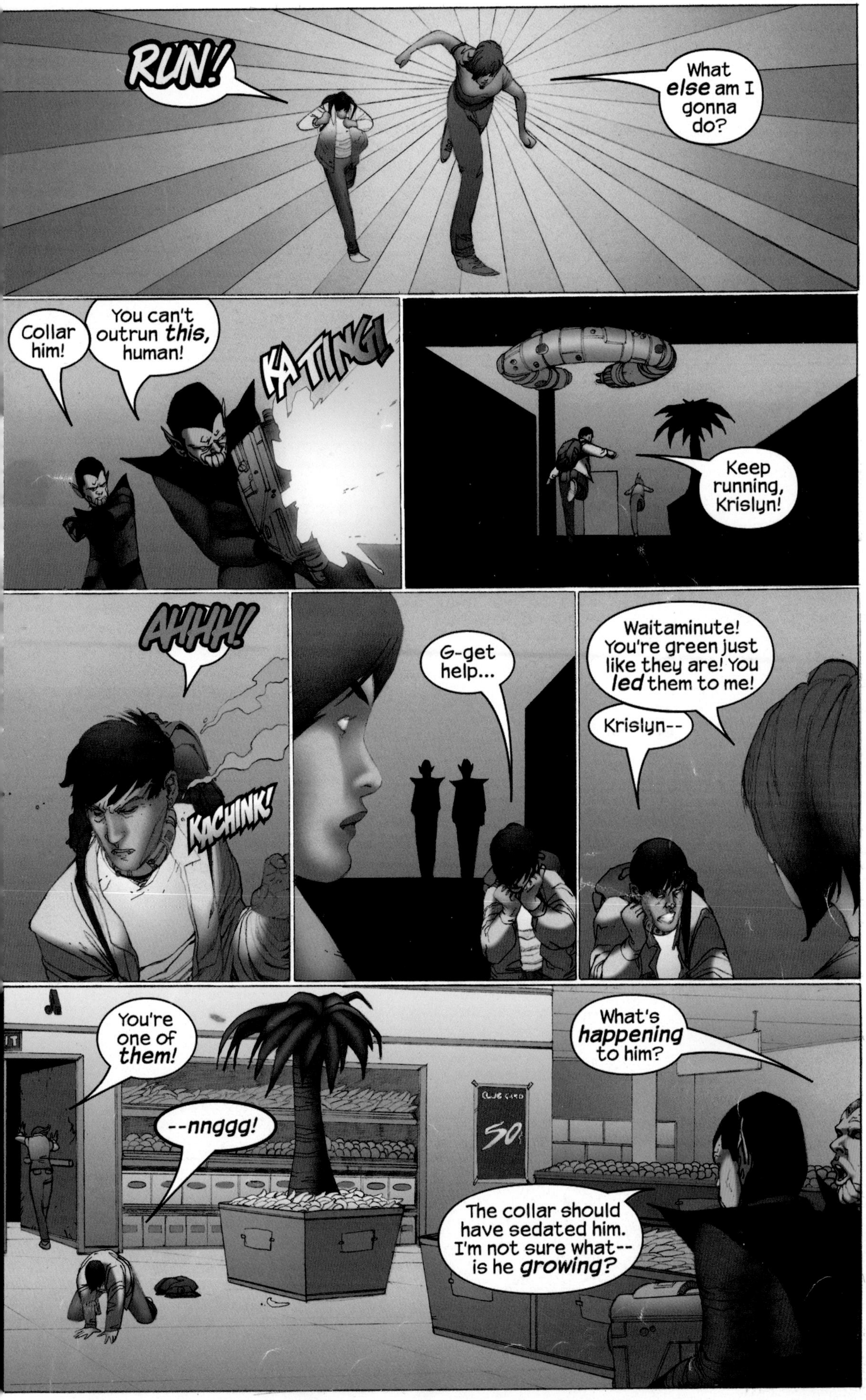
RUN!
What else am I gonna do?
Collar him!
You can't outrun this, human!
KA-TING!
Keep running, Krislyn!
AHHH!
KACHINK!
G-get help...
Waitaminute! You're green just like they are! You led them to me!
Krislyn--
You're one of them!
--nnggg!
What's happening to him?
The collar should have sedated him. I'm not sure what-- is he growing?
CLUB CARD
50¢

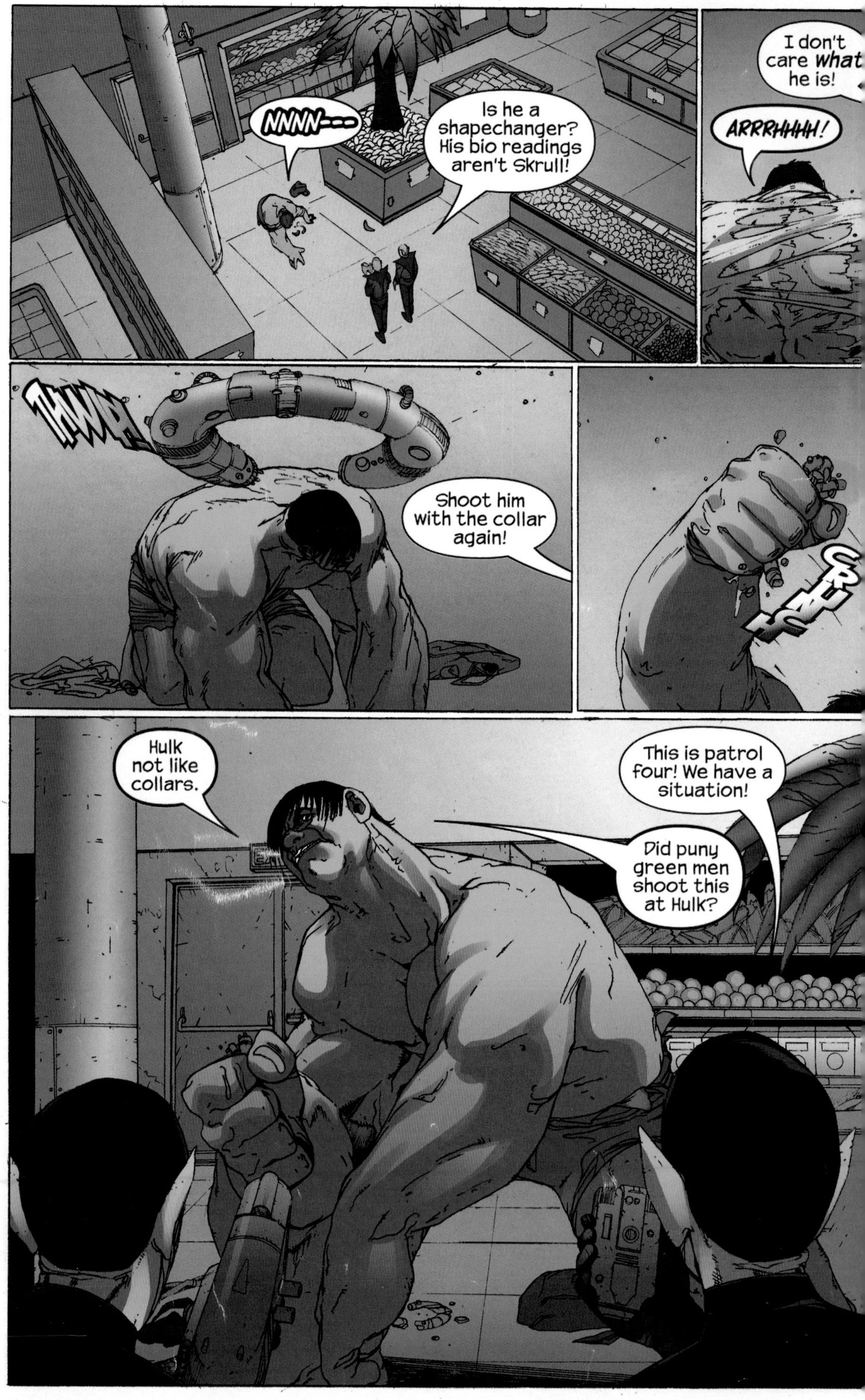
NNNN---
Is he a shapechanger? His bio readings aren't Skrull!
I don't care what he is!
ARRRHHHH!
Shoot him with the collar again!
Hulk not like collars.
This is patrol four! We have a situation!
Did puny green men shoot this at Hulk?

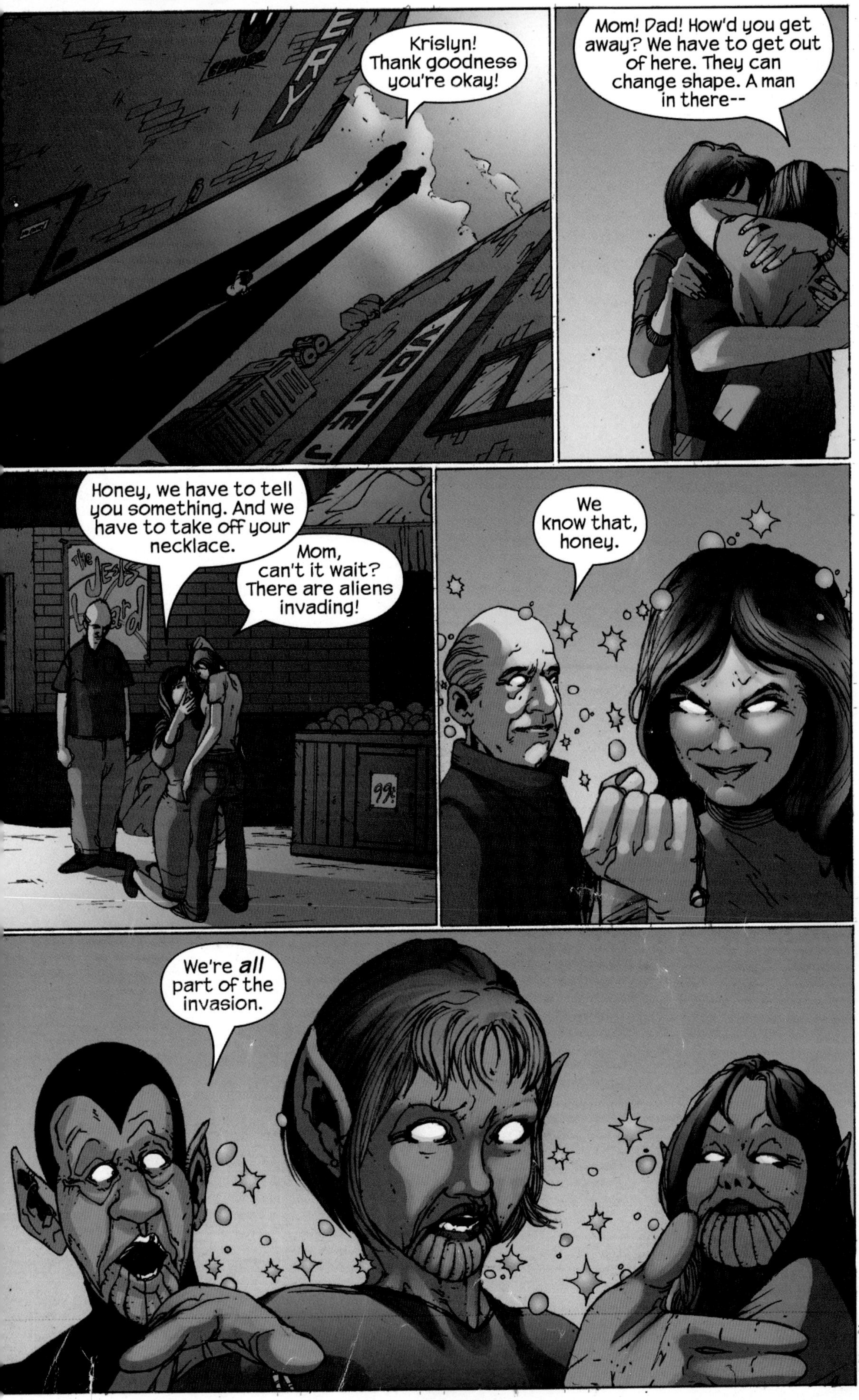
Krislyn! Thank goodness you're okay!
Mom! Dad! How'd you get away? We have to get out of here. They can change shape. A man in there--
Honey, we have to tell you something. And we have to take off your necklace.
Mom, can't it wait? There are aliens invading!
We know that, honey.
We're *all* part of the invasion.

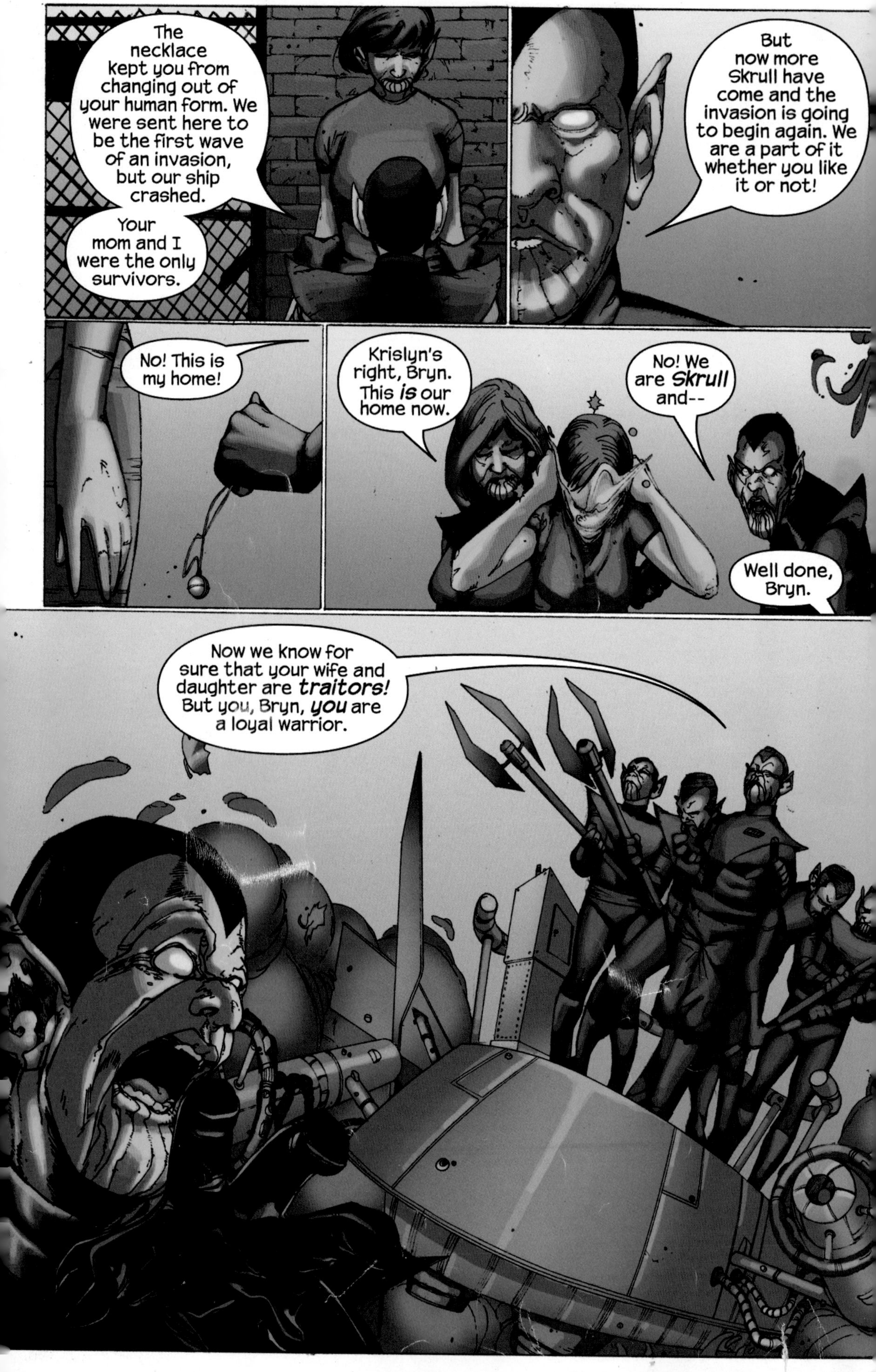

The necklace kept you from changing out of your human form. We were sent here to be the first wave of an invasion, but our ship crashed.
Your mom and I were the only survivors.
But now more Skrull have come and the invasion is going to begin again. We are a part of it whether you like it or not!
No! This is my home!
Krislyn's right, Bryn. This *is* our home now.
No! We are *Skrull* and--
Well done, Bryn.
Now we know for sure that your wife and daughter are *traitors!* But you, Bryn, *you* are a loyal warrior.

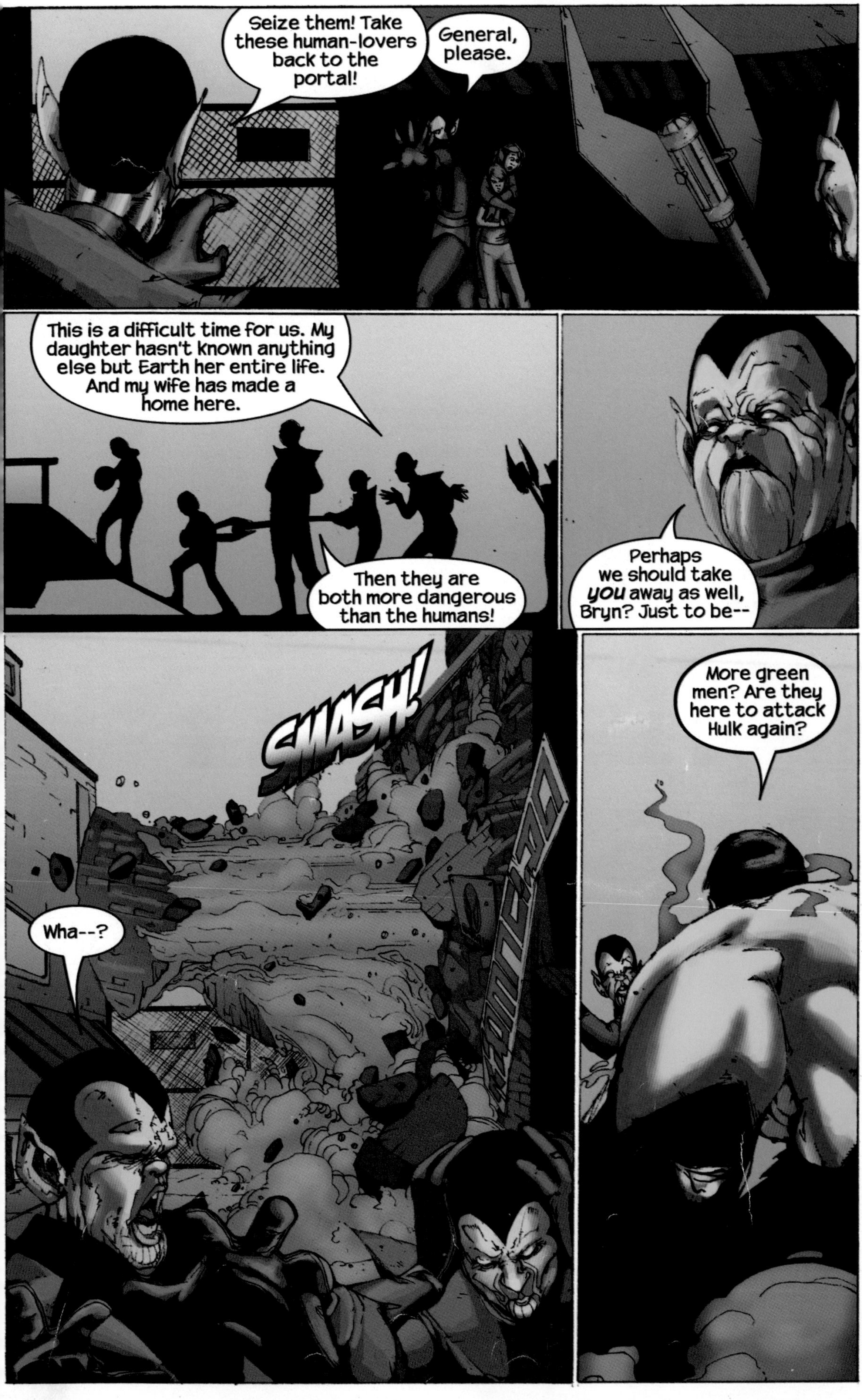
Seize them! Take these human-lovers back to the portal!
General, please.
This is a difficult time for us. My daughter hasn't known anything else but Earth her entire life. And my wife has made a home here.
Then they are both more dangerous than the humans!
Perhaps we should take *you* away as well, Bryn? Just to be--
SMASH!
Wha--?
More green men? Are they here to attack Hulk again?

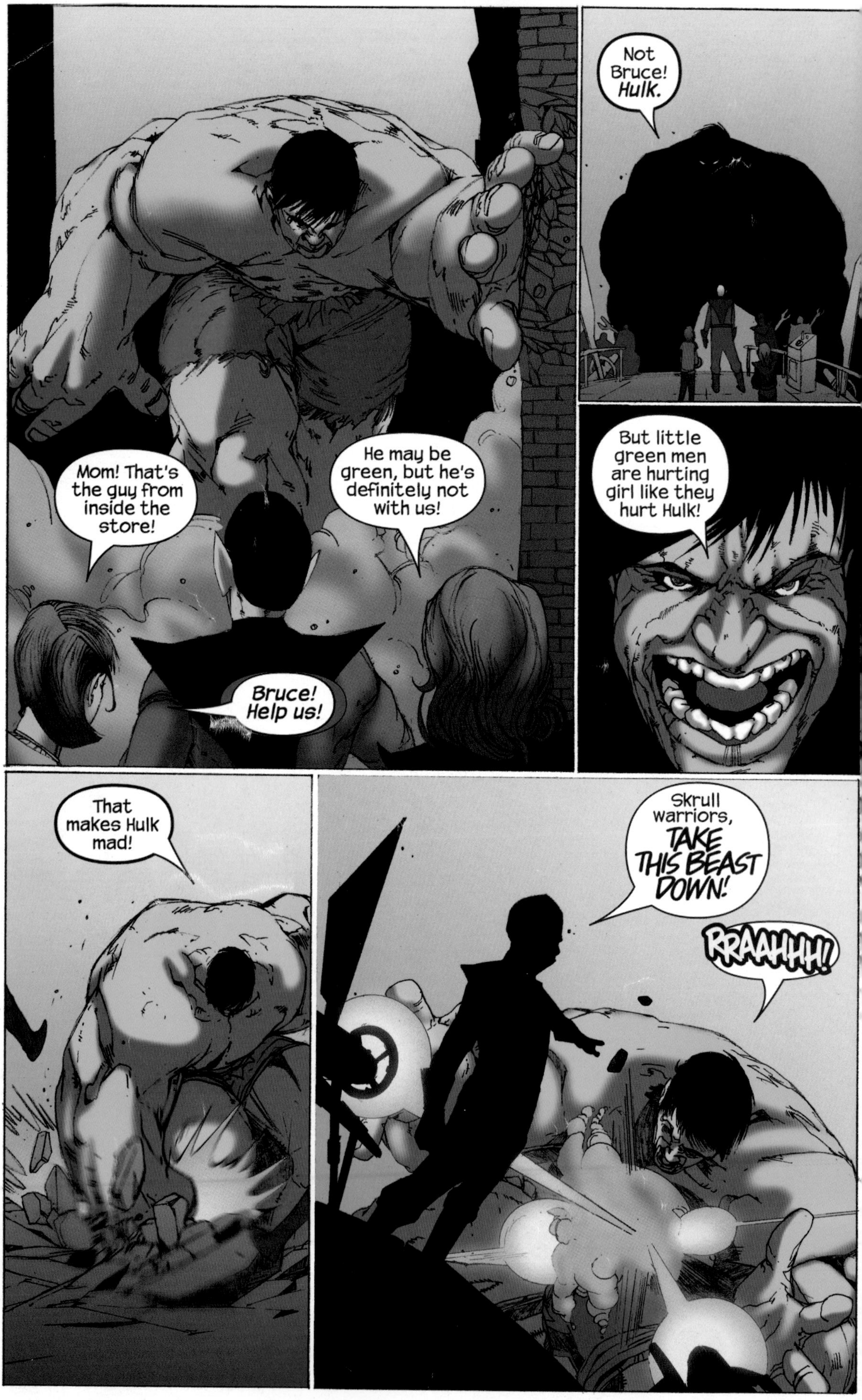
Mom! That's the guy from inside the store!
He may be green, but he's definitely not with us!
Bruce! Help us!
Not Bruce! Hulk.
But little green men are hurting girl like they hurt Hulk!
That makes Hulk mad!
Skrull warriors, TAKE THIS BEAST DOWN!
RRAAHHH!

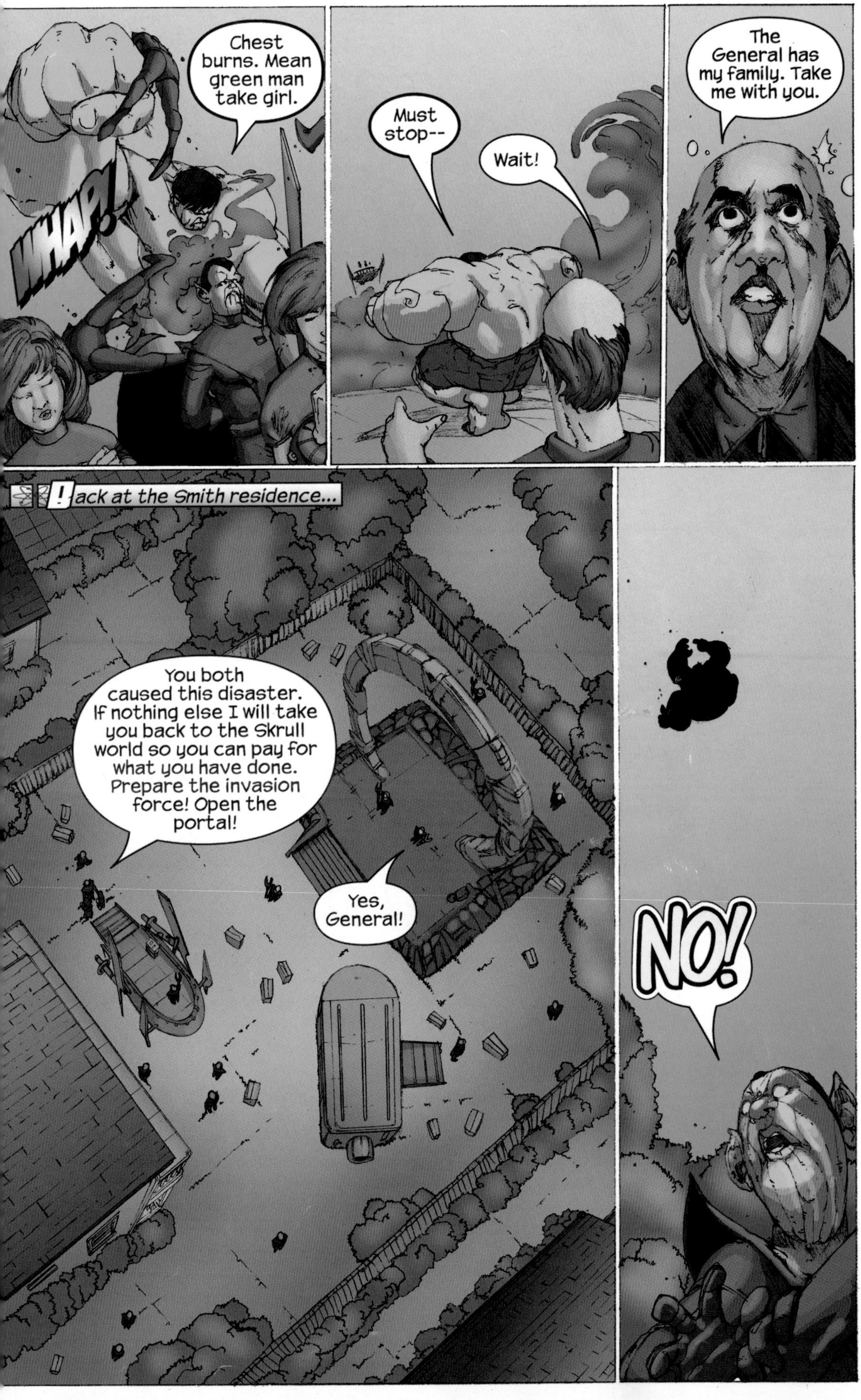
WHAP!
Chest burns. Mean green man take girl.
Must stop--
Wait!
The General has my family. Take me with you.
Back at the Smith residence...
You both caused this disaster. If nothing else I will take you back to the Skrull world so you can pay for what you have done. Prepare the invasion force! Open the portal!
Yes, General!
NO!

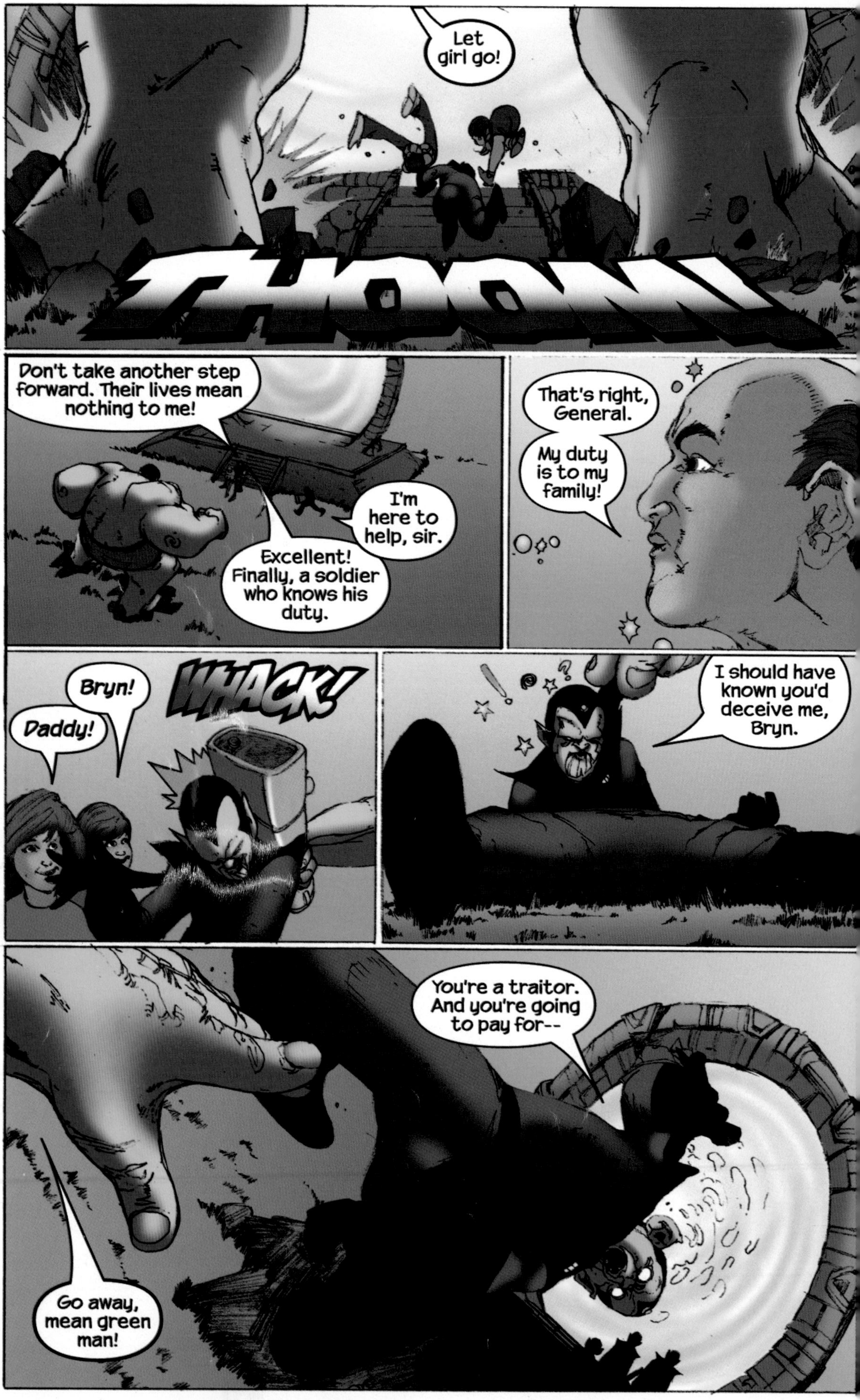
Let girl go!
THOOM!
Don't take another step forward. Their lives mean nothing to me!
I'm here to help, sir.
Excellent! Finally, a soldier who knows his duty.
That's right, General.
My duty is to my family!
Bryn!
Daddy!
WHACK!
I should have known you'd deceive me, Bryn.
You're a traitor. And you're going to pay for--
Go away, mean green man!

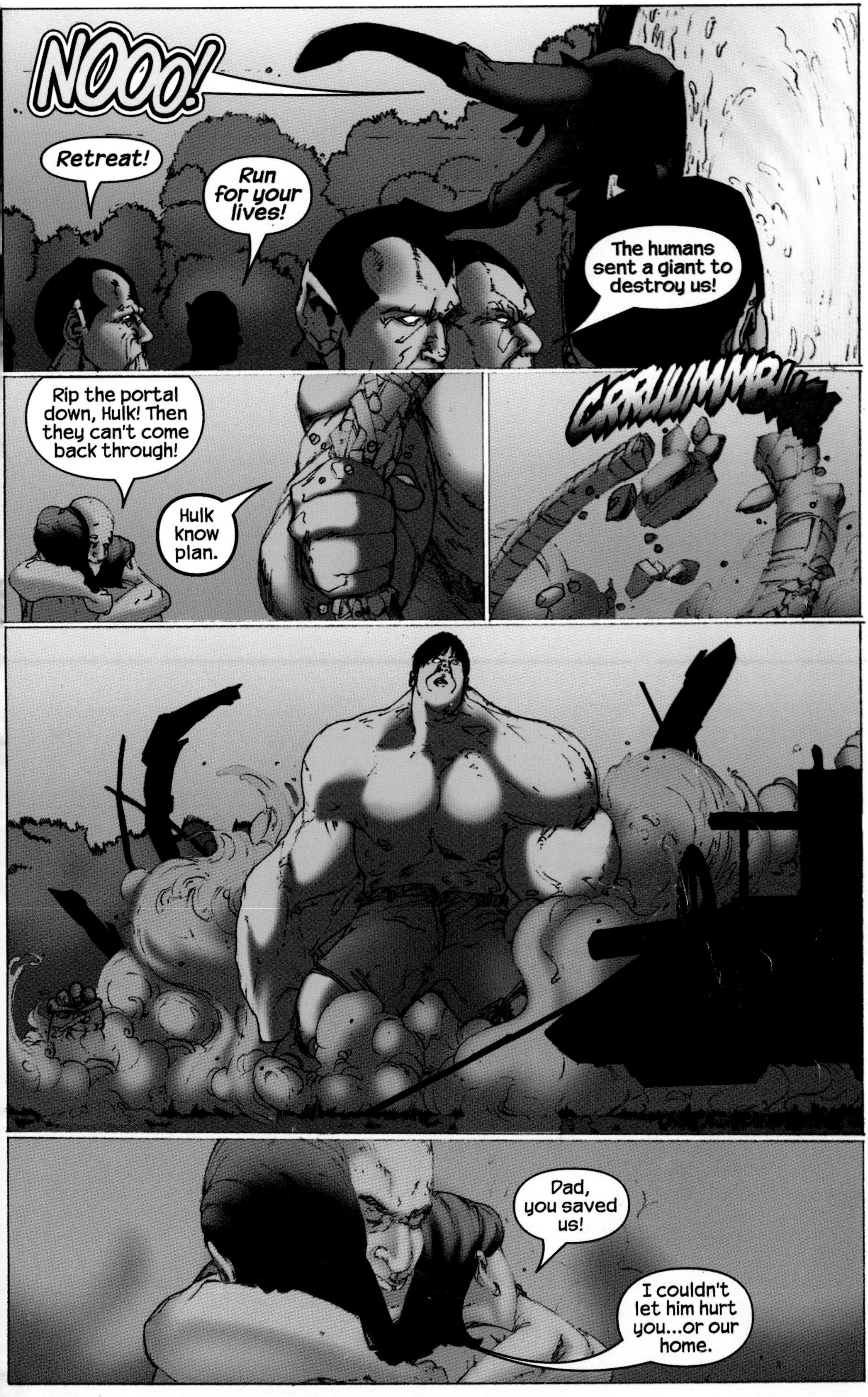
NOOO!
Retreat!
Run for your lives!
The humans sent a giant to destroy us!
Rip the portal down, Hulk! Then they can't come back through!
Hulk know plan.
CRRUMMBL
Dad, you saved us!
I couldn't let him hurt you...or our home.

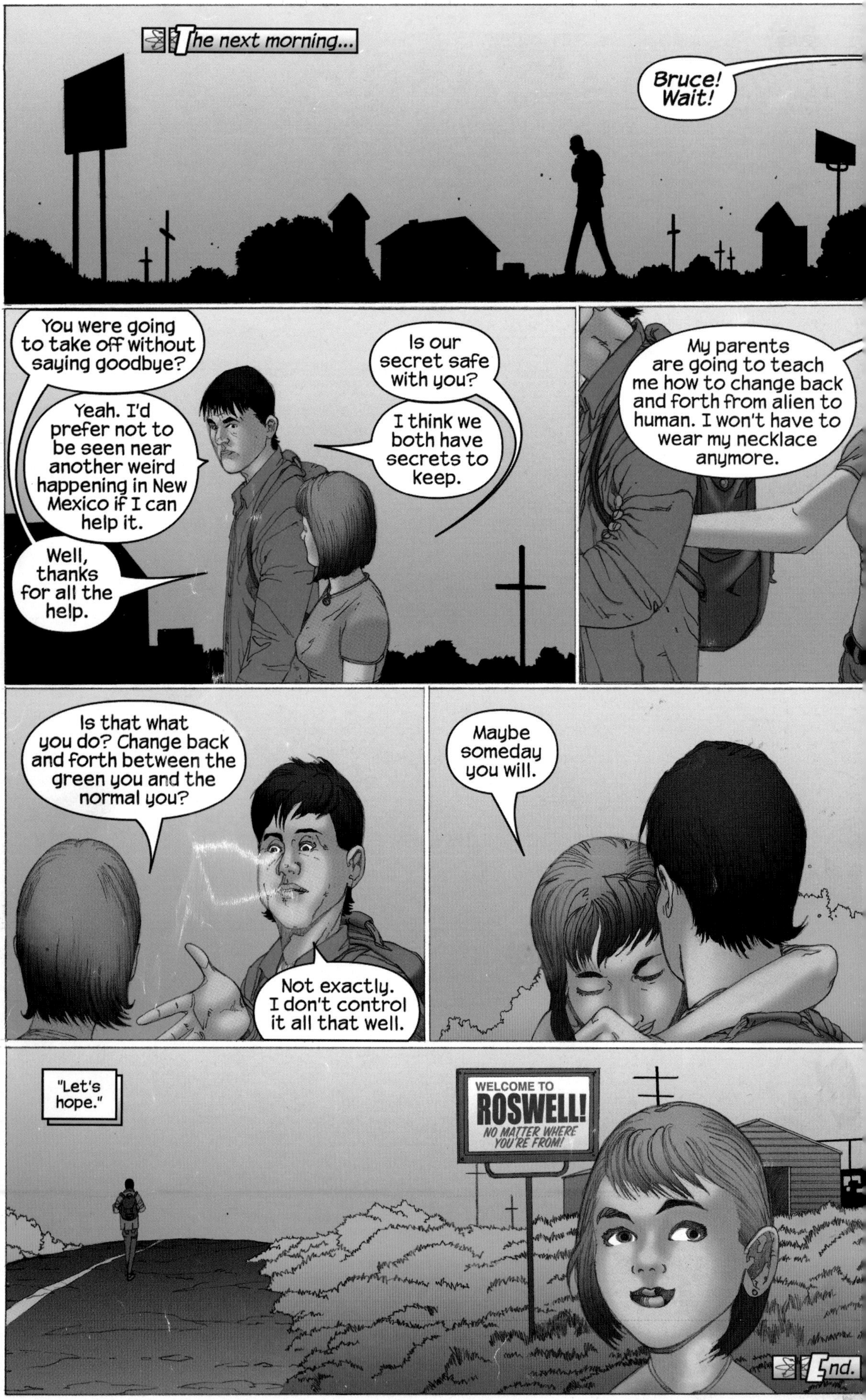
The next morning...
Bruce! Wait!
You were going to take off without saying goodbye?
Yeah. I'd prefer not to be seen near another weird happening in New Mexico if I can help it.
Well, thanks for all the help.
Is our secret safe with you?
I think we both have secrets to keep.
My parents are going to teach me how to change back and forth from alien to human. I won't have to wear my necklace anymore.
Is that what you do? Change back and forth between the green you and the normal you?
Not exactly. I don't control it all that well.
Maybe someday you will.
"Let's hope."
WELCOME TO
ROSWELL!
NO MATTER WHERE YOU'RE FROM!
End.